MYTHICAL CREATURES
CENTAURS

BY THOMAS KINGSLEY TROUPE

BELLWETHER MEDIA • MINNEAPOLIS, MN

Torque brims with excitement perfect for thrill-seekers of all kinds. Discover daring survival skills, explore uncharted worlds, and marvel at mighty engines and extreme sports. In *Torque* books, anything can happen. Are you ready?

This edition first published in 2021 by Bellwether Media, Inc.

No part of this publication may be reproduced in whole or in part without written permission of the publisher.
For information regarding permission, write to Bellwether Media, Inc.,
Attention: Permissions Department,
6012 Blue Circle Drive, Minnetonka, MN 55343.

Library of Congress Cataloging-in-Publication Data

Names: Troupe, Thomas Kingsley, author.
Title: Centaurs / by Thomas Kingsley Troupe.
Description: Minneapolis, MN : Bellwether Media, 2021. | Series: Torque |
  Includes bibliographical references and index. | Audience: Ages 7-12 |
  Audience: Grades 4-6 | Summary: "Engaging images accompany information
  about centaurs. The combination of high-interest subject matter and
  light text is intended for students in grades 3 through 7"-Provided by
  publisher.
Identifiers: LCCN 2020014865 (print) | LCCN 2020014866 (ebook) | ISBN
  9781644872727 | ISBN 9781681037356 (ebook)
Subjects: LCSH: Centaurs–Juvenile literature.
Classification: LCC BL820.C37 K56 2021 (print) | LCC BL820.C37 (ebook) |
  DDC 398/.45–dc23 LC record available at https://lccn.loc.gov/2020014865LC
ebook record available at https://lccn.loc.gov/2020014866

Text copyright © 2021 by Bellwether Media, Inc. TORQUE and associated logos are trademarks and/or registered trademarks of Bellwether Media, Inc.

Editor: Rebecca Sabelko   Designer: Josh Brink

Printed in the United States of America, North Mankato, MN.

TABLE OF CONTENTS

THE LEGEND OF A MYTHICAL BEAST	4
FRIEND OR FOE?	10
INSPIRING CREATURES	16
GLOSSARY	22
TO LEARN MORE	23
INDEX	24

THE LEGEND OF A MYTHICAL BEAST

The earth shakes. Tree branches snap on the forest floor. A group of centaurs races through the woods.

The sound of their hooves comes to a sudden halt. Soon, the group circles an **intruder**. They draw their arrows. There is no way to escape!

Centaurs are creatures from Greek **mythology**. They have the head and upper body of a human. They also have the body of a horse. Some have pointy ears. They can also have horns.

Greek myths state that these beasts were born from the **mares** of Mount Pelion. They roamed the forests of Thessaly.

Centaur Origin

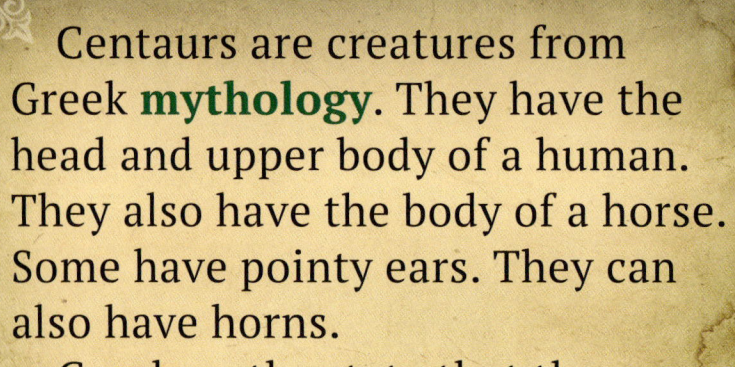

Thessaly, Greece =

Centaurs in Greek myths are often wild and **violent**. They refuse to follow the rules of man. The creatures act more like animals than humans.

Similar Creatures

sphinx

mermaid

chimera

faun

Minotaur

Stories say that centaurs live in caves. The beasts form tribes in some tales. They hunt animals using sticks and rocks. They eat raw meat.

FRIEND OR FOE?

bull hunting

Many believe the first centaur stories were spoken myths. These tales may have been based on the **tradition** of bull hunting during the **Bronze Age**.

Bull Hunters

Some believe the word *centaur* really means "bull killer."

In Thessaly, bull hunters were skilled horsemen. The hunters and horses worked so well together, they may have appeared as one creature.

Human images became popular on Greek pottery during the 900s BCE. Some artwork included centaur figures. These creatures were often shown fighting battles against gods or heroes.

Before long, they were mentioned in writing. Homer wrote of beasts during the 700s BCE. Many people believe he was referring to centaurs. Pindar described the creatures around 500 BCE. He wrote about peaceful creatures who roamed the forests.

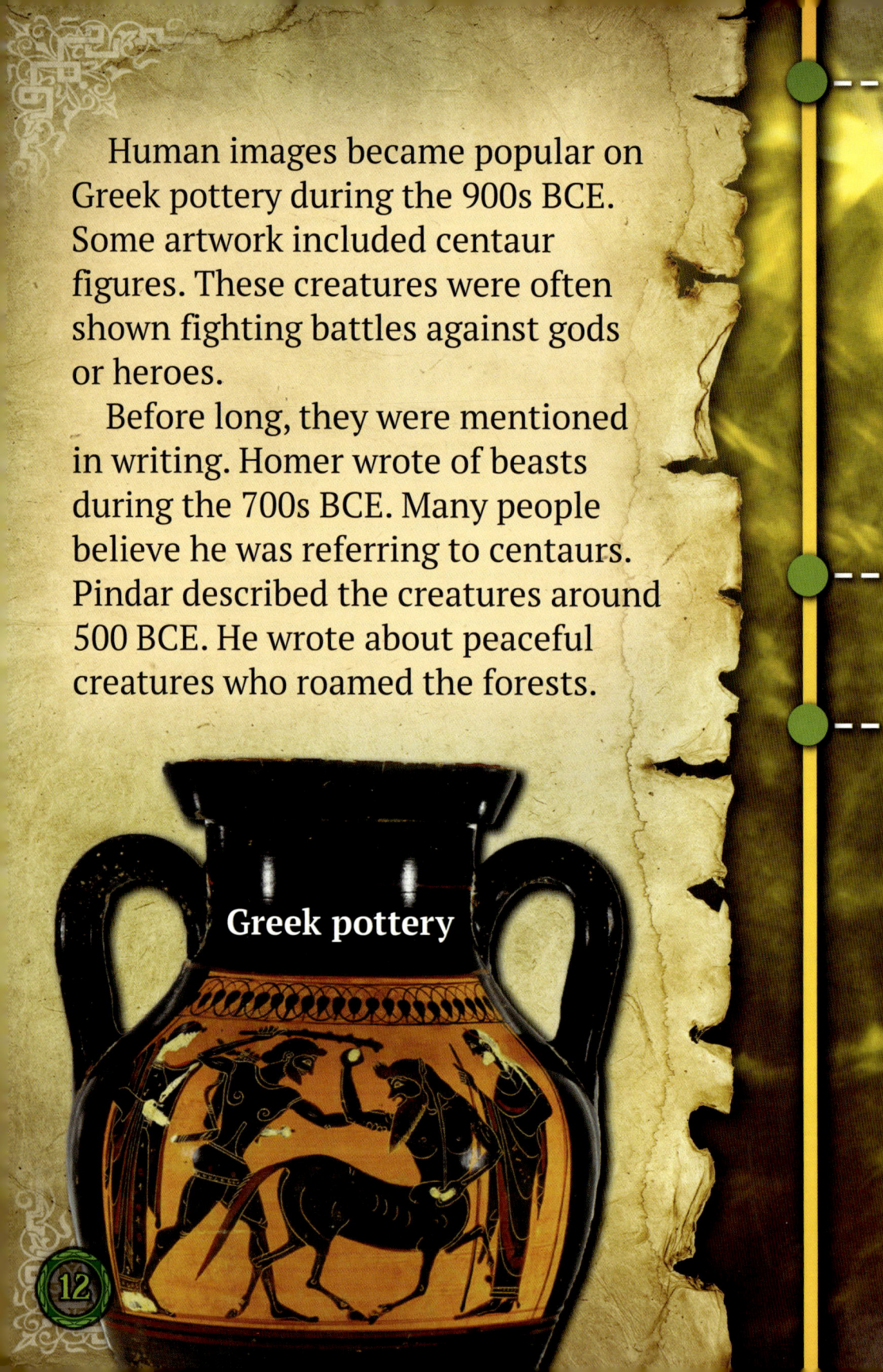

Greek pottery

Centaur Timeline

around 3000 BCE: Greek myths about centaurs begin with spoken stories

950 BCE: A centaur sculpture is created in Lefkandi, Greece

700s BCE: Homer writes about a centaur-like beast in the *Iliad*

These mythical creatures took on different behaviors from story to story. Some were friendly and helped humans. A famous helpful centaur is Chiron. He trained young men in medicine and music. He prepared heroes for warfare.

Most often, these half-human, half-horse creatures became violent in tales. The creatures fought humans. They caused trouble and damage. They angered the gods.

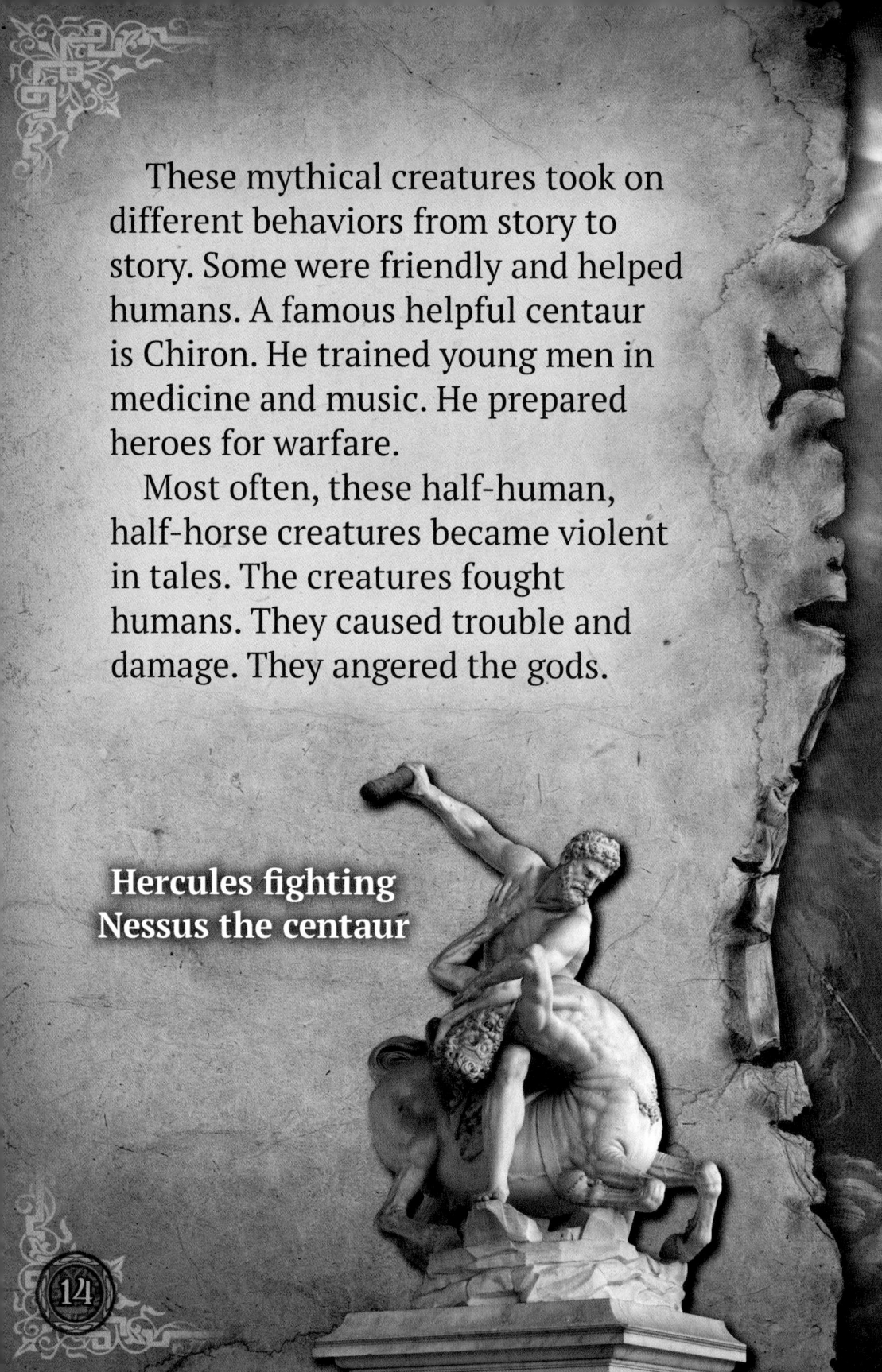

Hercules fighting Nessus the centaur

Forever in the Stars

The Greeks named a group of stars for Chiron. The group is called Centaurus.

Chiron

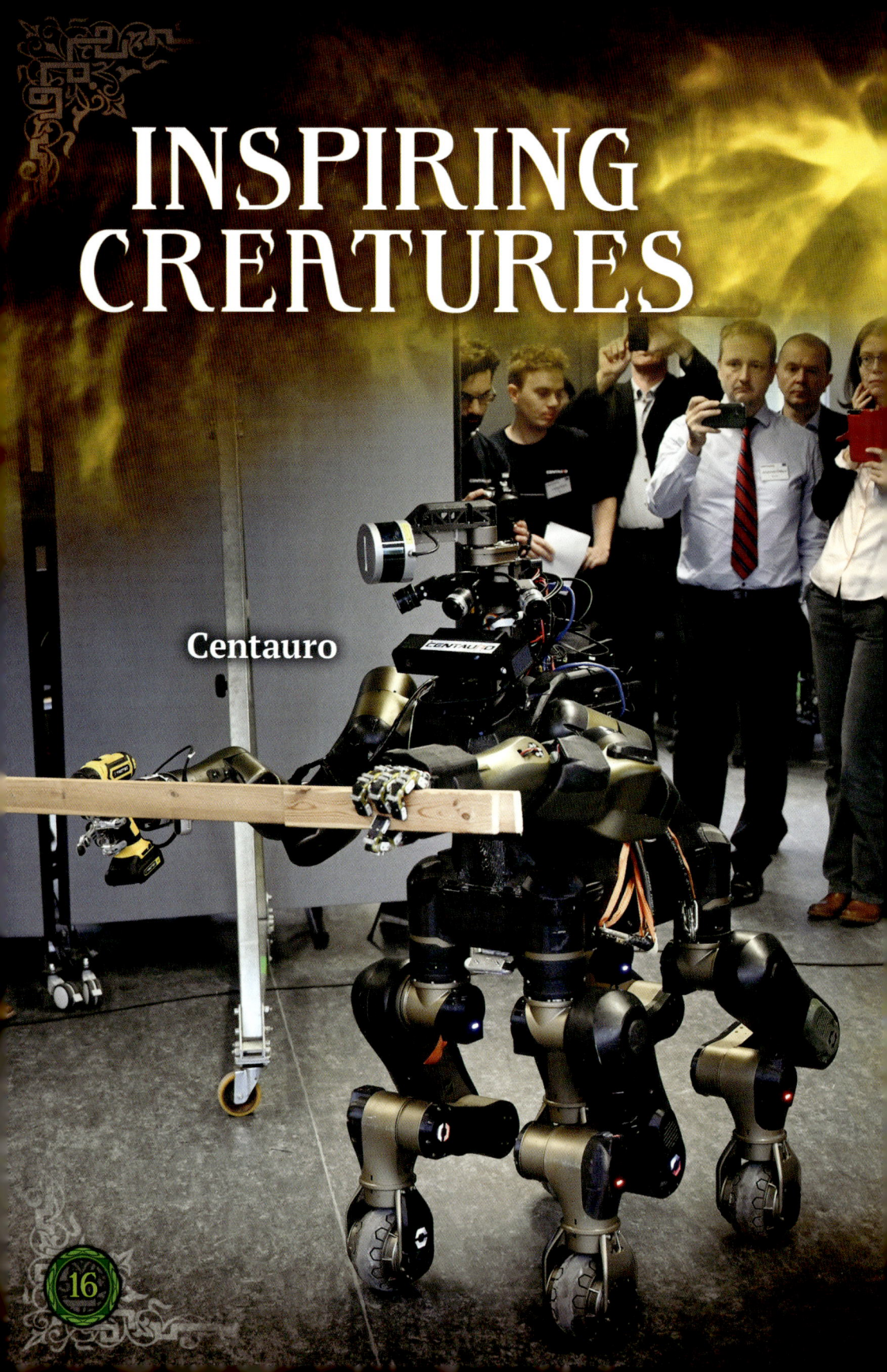

INSPIRING CREATURES

Centauro

Today, these mythical creatures still **inspire** people. Scientists created a robot centaur at the Italian Institute of Technology in 2018. It is called Centauro.

   This robot has four legs and an upper body with arms. It is built to enter disaster areas that are too dangerous for people!

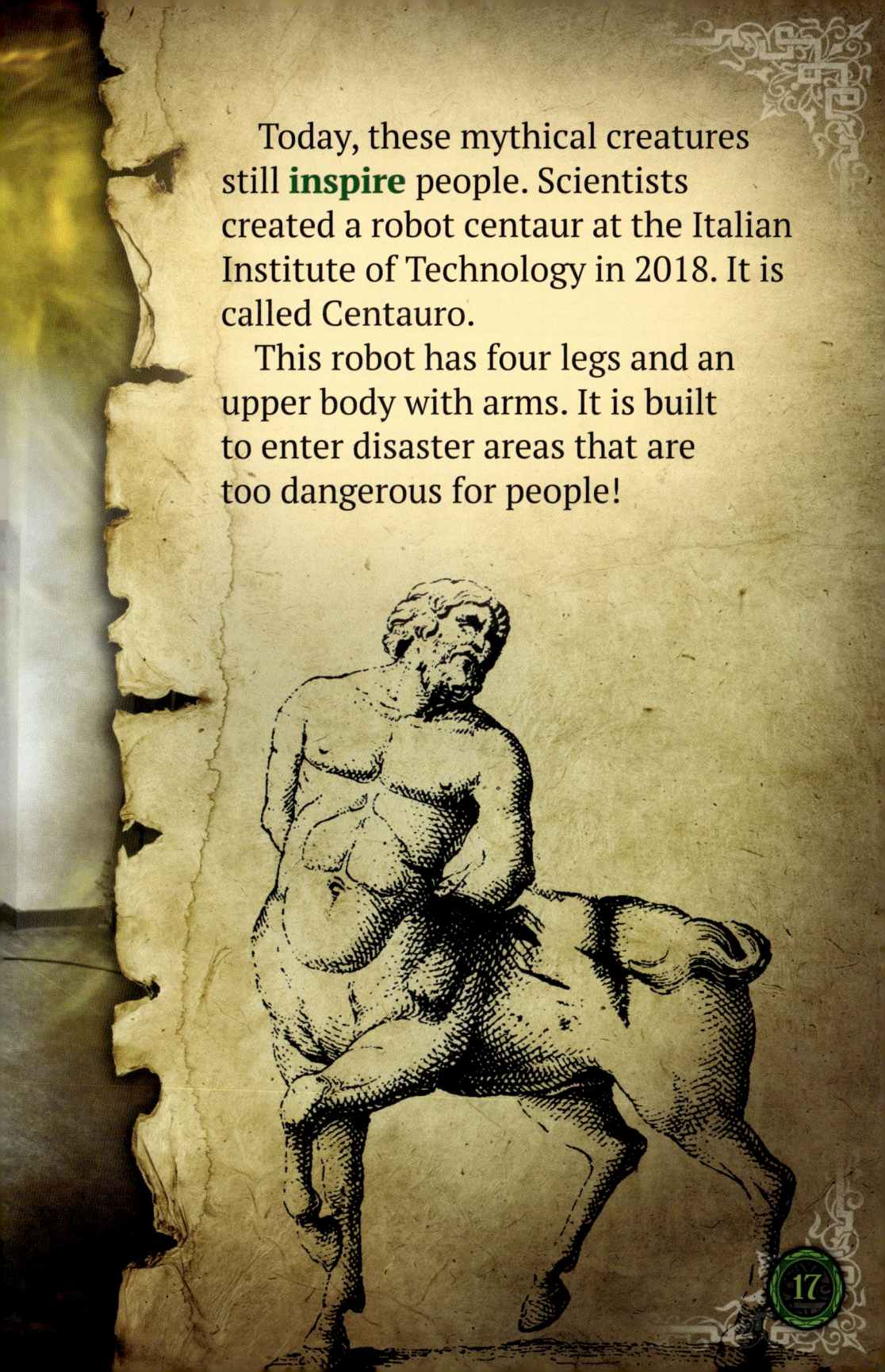

Centaurs continue to appear as wild creatures in media. They are often friendly in the Harry Potter series. But they can become dangerous when they are wronged.

Glenstorm

They also appear as friendly creatures in many of today's films. A centaur named Glenstorm appeared in the 2008 film *The Chronicles of Narnia: Prince Caspian*. He is a loyal warrior and **astronomer**.

Media Mention

Book Series: Percy Jackson and the Olympians

Years Released: 2005 to 2009

Character: Chiron is a centaur and the activities director at Camp Half-Blood

Powers: speed, healer, alters memories

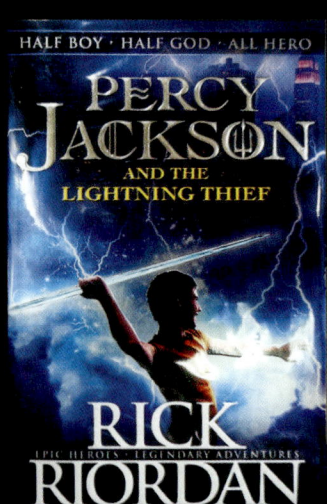

Percy Jackson: Sea of Monsters

These mythical creatures are also featured in other forms of media. Foaly from the Artemis Fowl books is an inventor. He creates helpful **gadgets**. A Lynel is a dangerous enemy in *The Legend of Zelda: Breath of the Wild* video game. It uses its intelligence to fight the main character, Link.

This fantastic mythical creature is thousands of years old. But it still inspires people today!

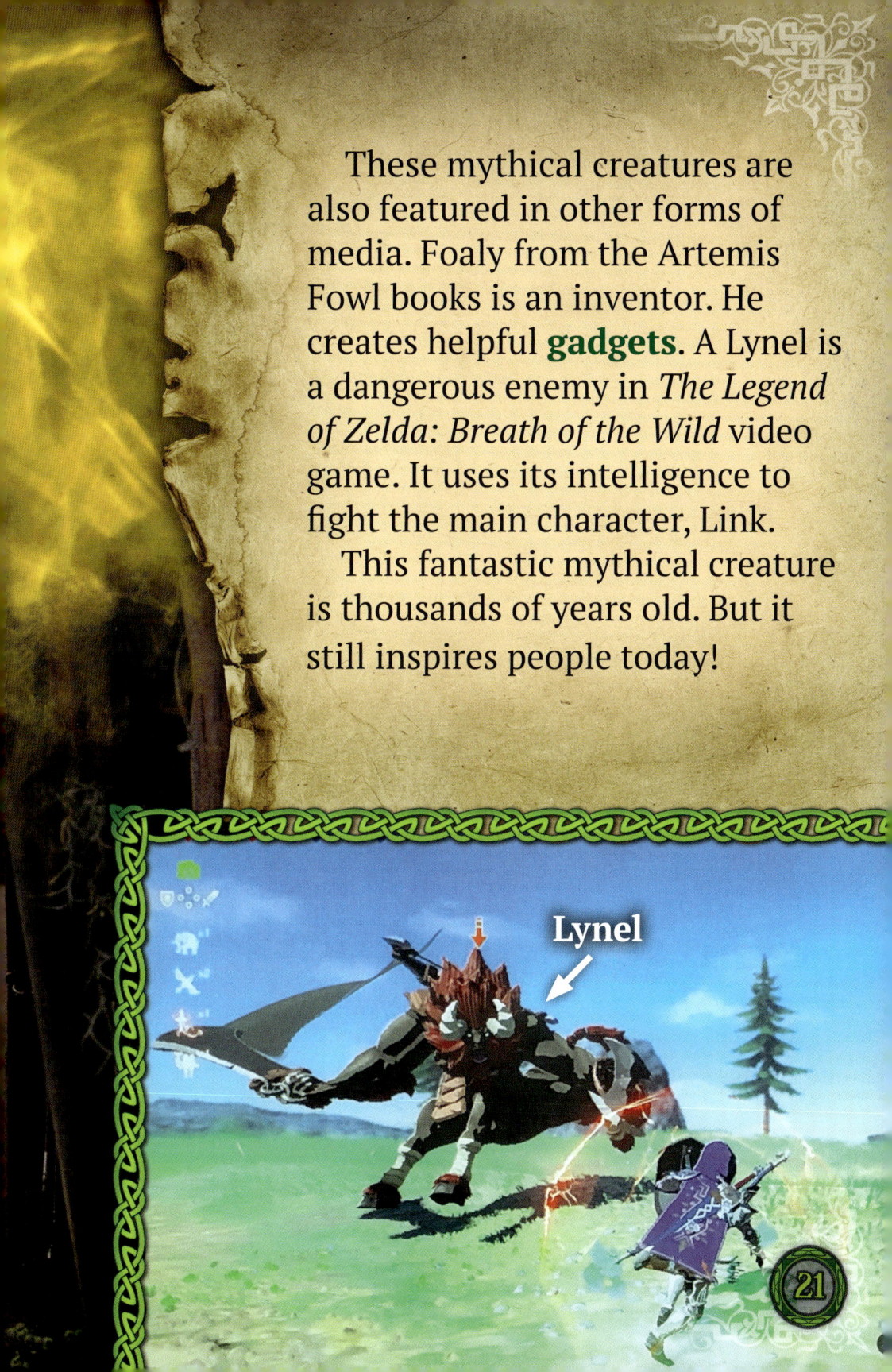

Lynel

GLOSSARY

astronomer—someone who studies space

Bronze Age—the period of history from about 3000 to 1100 BCE

gadgets—small, unusual devices with particular uses

inspire—to give someone an idea about what to do or create

intruder—someone who is not welcome

mares—female horses

mythology—ancient stories about the beliefs or history of a group of people; myths also try to explain events.

tradition—a custom, idea, or belief handed down from one generation to the next

violent—using physical force to cause harm to someone or something

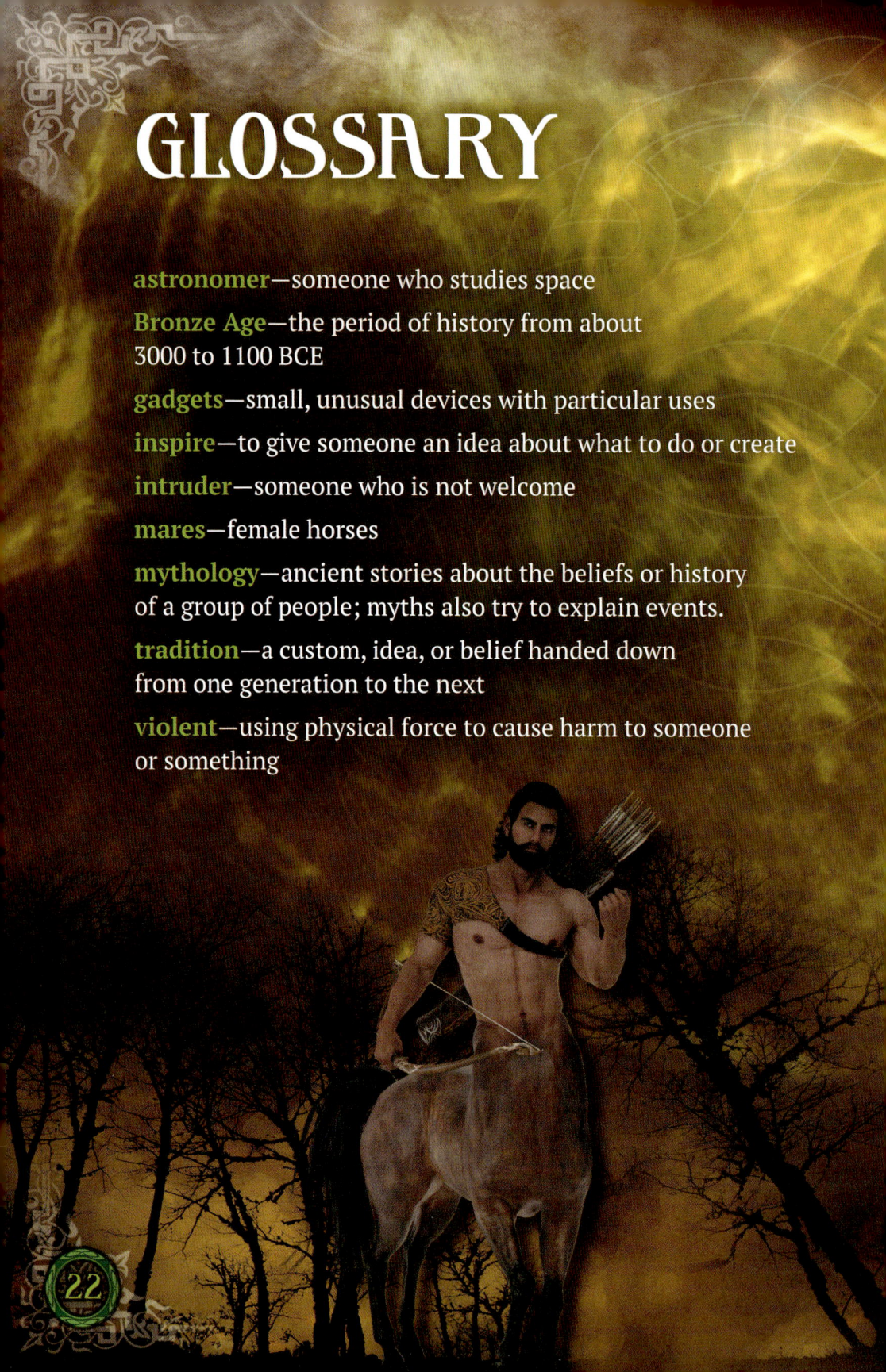

TO LEARN MORE

AT THE LIBRARY

Briggs, Korwin. *Gods and Heroes: Mythology Around the World*. New York, N.Y.: Workman Publishing Co., 2018.

Flynn, Sarah Wassner. *Greek Mythology*. Washington, D.C.: National Geographic, 2018.

Lawrence, Sandra, and Stuart Hill. *The Atlas of Monsters: Mythical Creatures from Around the World*. Philadelphia, Pa.: Running Press Kids, 2019.

ON THE WEB

FACTSURFER

Factsurfer.com gives you a safe, fun way to find more information.

1. Go to www.factsurfer.com

2. Enter "centaurs" into the search box and click 🔍.

3. Select your book cover to see a list of related content.

INDEX

appearance, 6

Artemis Fowl (series), 21

astronomer, 19

Bronze Age, 10

bull hunting, 10, 11

centauresses, 5

Centauro, 16, 17

Chiron, 14, 15

Chronicles of Narnia, The: Prince Caspian, 19

Foaly, 21

Glenstorm, 19

gods, 12, 14

Greece, 5, 6, 8, 12, 15

Harry Potter (series), 18

heroes, 12, 14

history, 10, 11, 12, 17

Homer, 12

human, 6, 8, 12, 14

Italian Institute of Technology, 17

Legend of Zelda, The: Breath of the Wild, 21

Mount Pelion, 6

mythology, 6, 8, 10

origin, 6, 10, 11

Percy Jackson and the Olympians, 20

Pindar, 12

pottery, 12

similar creatures, 9

Thessaly, 6, 11

timeline, 12-13

tradition, 10

The images in this book are reproduced through the courtesy of: Elnur, front cover (human hero); mariait, front cover (horse hero); stockfotoart, front cover (background); Algol, p. 3; Paul Aniszewski, p. 3 (background); dugdax, pp. 4-5 (background); Google Cultural Institute/ Wiki Commons, pp. 6-7; The Print Collector/ Alamy, pp. 8-9; Olaf Krüger/ Alamy, p. 9 (sphinx)(chimera); Science History Images/ Alamy, p. 9 (mermaid); Albatross/ Alamy, p. 9 (faun); Artur Balytskyi/ Alamy, p. 9 (minotaur); Chronicle/ Alamy, pp. 10-11; Artokoloro/ Alamy, pp. 12-13; World History Archive/ Alamy, p. 13 (top); DEA Picture Library/ Getty, p. 13 (middle); Marie-Lan Nguyen/ Wiki Commons, p. 13 (bottom); Azoor Photo/ Alamy, p. 14; Pictures Now/ Alamy, pp. 14-15; picture alliance/ Getty, pp. 16-17; Morphart Creation, p. 17; TCD/Prod.DB/ Alamy, pp. 18-19; 20th Century Fox/ Alamy, pp. 20-21; Betsy Rathburn, p. 21; TreesTons, p. 22; Francisco Caravana, p. 22 (background).